5.3

# JULIA ROBERTS

by
Jill C. Wheeler

# Visit us at
# www.abdopub.com

Published by ABDO Publishing Company, 4940 Viking
Drive, Edina, MN 55435. Copyright ©2001 by Abdo
Consulting Group, Inc. International copyrights reserved in
all countries. No part of this book may be reproduced in
any form without written permission from the publisher.

Printed in the United States.

Graphic Design: John Hamilton
Cover Design: MacLean Tuminelly
Cover photo: Shooting Stars
Interior photos:
   Amblin Entertainment and TriStar Pictures, p. 24
   AP/Wide World, p. 17, 18-19, 30, 39, 43, 51
   Corbis, p. 6, 10, 21, 33, 35, 40-41, 45, 47, 53, 55, 59,
      60-61, 63
   Jersey Films and Universal Pictures, p. 48
   Polygram Filmed Entertainment, p. 42
   Shooting Stars, p. 5, 9, 13, 15, 22, 25, 27, 57
   Time Pix, p. 7, 28, 36, 44, 49
   Touchstone Pictures and Paramount Pictures, p. 42

**Library of Congress Cataloging-in-Publication Data**
Wheeler, Jill C., 1964-
     Julia Roberts / Jill C. Wheeler.
          p. cm. — (Star tracks)
     Includes index.
     ISBN 1-57765-555-9
     1. Roberts, Julia, 1967—Juvenile literature.  2. Motion
picture actors and actresses—United States—Biography—
Juvenile literature. [1. Roberts, Julia, 1967-  2. Actors and
actresses.  3. Women—Biography.]  I. Title.  II. Series

PN2287.R63 W49 2001
791.43'028'092—dc21
[B]
                                                    00-050262

# CONTENTS

America's Sweetheart ........................................... 4

The Girl Next Door .............................................. 8

Winsome Waitress ............................................... 14

Personal Problems ............................................. 20

Where's Julia? .................................................. 26

Surprise Wedding .............................................. 32

Better Than Ever ............................................... 38

Wild About Erin ................................................ 46

Older & Wiser .................................................. 50

Flash That Smile ............................................... 56

Where On The Web? ........................................... 62

Glossary ....................................................... 63

Index .......................................................... 64

# AMERICA'S
# SWEETHEART

IT WAS 9:30 ON A MONDAY MORNING.
Students at Lenwood Elementary School in
Barstow, California, were expecting a day like any
other. Then a car pulled up carrying a special
visitor to the school.

The halls began to buzz almost as soon as the
tall young woman walked in. Everyone was
asking, "Is that *really* Julia Roberts?" The only
person who wasn't surprised was Lenwood
Principal Gerry Dame. The Friday before he had
invited the actress to visit the school. He knew
Julia was in Barstow to shoot her latest movie,
*Erin Brockovich*. He didn't hear back from her
however. He assumed she was too busy to stop by.

In all, Julia spent five hours at the school
visiting all 21 classes and talking with the
students. Many of the students there were from
low-income homes. They didn't usually get many
special treats. That day, they did.

*Julia Roberts greets fans at the 1999 Los Angeles premiere of her romantic comedy,* Runaway Bride.

Dame said Julia even helped serve lunch. "The next day I had parents calling saying, 'My kid just came home and said Julia Roberts was in the classroom, and we know he's making it up.' I had to say, 'No, she was really here.'

"We were all really smitten with her," Dame told *PEOPLE Magazine.* "It was obvious she wasn't here for the adults or to further some movie. She was here for the kids, to let them know that dreams do come true."

Julia's rise from a young unknown to her current spot as Hollywood's highest-paid actress *has* been a dream come true. Like anyone, she's had her ups and downs along the way. But her genuine, small-town roots also have made her America's sweetheart time and again.

**Julia's genuine, small-town roots have made her America's sweetheart.**

# THE GIRL

## NEXT DOOR

JULIA FIONA ROBERTS WAS BORN ON October 28, 1967, in Smyrna, Georgia, a small suburb of Atlanta. Her father, Walter, was a vacuum salesman. Her mother, Betty, was a church secretary. She has an older brother, Eric, and an older sister, Lisa.

Julia was born into a show business family. Her parents both were actors. They had conducted workshops for actors and playwrights before Julia was born. When Julia was still in a stroller, they would bring her with them when they performed Shakespeare in a local park.

*Julia at age eight.*

Walter and Betty divorced when Julia was four years old. Walter died of cancer when Julia was nine years old. "It had a profound effect on my life," she said of her father's death. "I think when you lose a parent as a young person, it takes away that dreamy quality of life that kids should be allowed."

As a child, Julia wanted to be a veterinarian— a tall veterinarian. When one of her teachers at Fitzhugh Lee Elementary School asked her what she wanted to be when she grew up, she said "Six feet tall." In truth she ended up close to that at 5-foot, 9-inches tall.

Julia says she had an average high school career. "I was considered completely common and average," she said. "I wasn't a good student. I wasn't a great speaker. I wasn't a great storyteller. I wasn't the funniest. I wasn't the most athletic. I wasn't any of those things."

# As a child, Julia was considered completely common and average.

Her classmates recall her as having a dramatic flair. "When we got bored, Jules could be real creative," said one friend. "She could muster up tears in a second to get out of homeroom. ..." Not surprisingly, she also was a finalist in the Campbell High School Miss Panthera beauty contest.

Three days after graduating from Campbell, 17-year-old Julia moved to New York to live with her sister, Lisa. Both Lisa and Julia's brother Eric were in the acting business. Julia wanted to follow suit. In the meantime, she signed up with the Click modeling agency to earn some cash. While her girl-next-door looks were fine for modeling, her heart wasn't in it. She still wanted to act.

Her brother helped with her first break. Eric already had picked up an Oscar nomination for his role in 1985's *Runaway Train*. He was set to star in a new drama called *Blood Red*. The script called for Eric to have a younger sister. He told the filmmakers that he had a younger sister, and could they give her the part? They agreed, and in 1986 Julia got her debut. Unfortunately, the film wasn't released to theaters until 1990.

"While her girl-next-door looks were fine for modeling, her heart wasn't in it. She still wanted to act."

# WINSOME
# WAITRESS

FOLLOWING *BLOOD RED*, JULIA BEGAN TO land other offers. Her professional debut came in 1988 when she won a part in an episode of *Crime Story* on NBC-TV. Then she won roles in three back-to-back movies. In *Satisfaction*, she played a teen-aged rocker alongside Liam Neeson. In the HBO comedy *Baja Oklahoma*, she played a rebel. And in *Mystic Pizza*, she stole hearts as Daisy, a Portuguese waitress working in a small-town pizzeria. Critics agreed Julia walked away with *Mystic Pizza*.

Her breakout performance in *Mystic Pizza* opened the door for Julia to land another big role. In *Steel Magnolias* she played Shelby Eatenton, a young bride who dies tragically from complications caused by her diabetes.

*Steel Magnolias* was set in a small southern town much like Julia's hometown. And while Julia had never finished an acting class, she had her own way of making her character's experiences into her own. It took work, however. "Challenge wise, it was like taking the SATs every day," she said of acting.

"I don't think (acting) lessons would have made much difference," said Robert Harling. Harling wrote the screenplay for *Steel Magnolias*. "She's just one of those people who's got it." Harling said Julia took her role of Shelby to heart—even when the character lay dying. "She came as close to death as you can while you're still alive," he said of Julia's final scene. "After every take, they'd have to pick her up and help her back to the trailer. She would just go all the way."

That dedication earned Julia an Oscar nomination and a Golden Globe Best Supporting Actress Award. It also gave her the confidence to pursue a new role. It was the role of Vivian Ward, a prostitute. When Julia won the role, the movie was to be a drama. Then Disney purchased the script. They changed it into a lighthearted romantic comedy. Julia didn't like the idea at first. She had wanted the dramatic challenge of the original concept. However, director Garry Marshall urged her to stick with the picture. The rest is history.

*Julia Roberts as Vivian Ward, in* **Pretty Woman.**

*Pretty Woman* was a smash, and Julia became an overnight sensation. Her performance even won her another Oscar nomination for Best Actress, as well as a Golden Globe best actress nomination. As with *Steel Magnolias*, the filming took a lot out of Julia. Reports from the set claimed she would break down and cry after tough scenes. Marshall said sometimes he needed to remind Julia that it was "just acting."

*Left: Julia Roberts with co-star Richard Gere in* Pretty Woman.

# PERSONAL

## P R O B L E M S

WITH HER STAR POWER ESTABLISHED, Julia moved from the romantic comedy of *Pretty Woman* to *Flatliners*. *Flatliners* is about medical students who experiment with near-death experiences. The movie co-starred Kiefer Sutherland, son of actor Donald Sutherland.

Even with such a somber topic, Julia brought a lighthearted spirit to the set. Once the director got her and the rest of the cast laughing. "I made Julia laugh so hard that I couldn't get her focused again," recalls director Joel Schumacher. "She'd be bending over the dying Kiefer and then suddenly start screaming with laughter."

The same year, Julia starred in *Sleeping With the Enemy,* about a woman who tries to leave her abusive husband.

# Even with somber topics, Julia brings a lighthearted spirit to the set.

Meanwhile, things in Julia's personal life were heating up. She had been romantically linked before with her co-stars. She lived together for a while with *Satisfaction* co-star Liam Neeson. She also had been engaged to *Magnolias* on-screen husband Dylan McDermott. She broke that engagement after she met Kiefer on the *Flatliners* set. Now she frequently was seen with him. It wasn't long before the Hollywood tabloids were talking about a wedding for Julia and Kiefer. It was to take place on June 14, 1991.

On June 10, Julia's and Kiefer's publicists announced the wedding was off. The news took Hollywood by storm. Workers had nearly completed transforming 20th Century Fox Soundstage 14 into a garden paradise for the wedding. Now the workers began to dismantle it. On the day the wedding was to have taken place, Julia hopped a jet to Ireland. She was with longtime friend Jason Patric.

The rumors began almost immediately. Had Julia left Kiefer because of Jason? Or were they just friends? Other rumors said Kiefer had been romantically involved with a local dancer. One week later, Julia's new movie opened in theaters. *Dying Young* was a sad film that didn't do well at the box office.

To top that off, Julia was to start work with Steven Spielberg on the movie *Hook*. *Hook* was a re-telling of the Peter Pan story. Julia was to play Tinkerbell. As filming began, stories circulated about Julia's problem behavior on the *Hook* set. She often was moody and would lock herself in her trailer between takes. After *Hook* wrapped, the highest paid actress in Hollywood virtually disappeared from the entertainment scene.

# WHERE'S JULIA?

HOLLYWOOD INSIDERS GUESSED JULIA was having a hard time handling being famous. At only 23 years of age, it was tough to be in the spotlight all the time. Her personal life was anything but private. "There are photographers who sit in their cars outside my house all day long…" Julia told a reporter.

To friends, Julia dreamed of a life where she wouldn't be recognized everywhere she went. She also dreamed of a time when her every move wouldn't be reported in the newspapers. "It's bizarre to deal with reports in the press about my romantic life," Julia told another reporter. "I've read flat-out lies so hideous they made me cry."

Julia continued to review scripts during her time off. However she didn't find any that she wanted to pursue. She used her extra time to visit her mother back in Georgia and do some traveling.

Back in Hollywood,
Julia continued to
be in the spotlight.

In February 1992, Julia traveled to Calcutta, India. She spent two weeks working at one of Mother Teresa's missions for children. "Going to India was extraordinary," she said. "It really sort of puts you back into place… It really snaps you into a place of perspective that doesn't really exist in the day-to-day world."

Back in Hollywood, she continued to be in the spotlight. When she was seen in public, there almost certainly was a story about it the next week. Reports on her personal life said she had broken up with Jason Patric so she could date Daniel Day-Lewis. Other reports had her out on the town with Sean Penn.

During her 18-months away from making movies, she made just one film appearance. It was a short cameo in *The Player*. *The Player* is a film about the Hollywood movie industry. Julia was set to star in *Shakespeare in Love*. She walked off that set when she learned Day-Lewis would not be her co-star.

*Julia Roberts, who visited Haiti and worked with disadvantaged youths there, accepted an award in 1996 from the Haitian Consulate in Boston for her outstanding activism in support of Haiti.*

Many in the film industry criticized her for dropping out of the business. They felt her career could not recover from such an absence. "It's not that the bloom is off Julia Roberts," said one producer. "It's just that she's going to have to gain momentum again. This really is a town of who's the flavor of the month."

Many in the film
industry criticized
Julia for dropping
out of the business.

King's Ridge Christian School
Media Center

# SURPRISE
## WEDDING

JULIA STEPPED BACK INTO THE SPOTLIGHT with a whirlwind romance and surprise wedding. She met country singer Lyle Lovett in June 1993. Three weeks later, on June 27, 1993, they were married in a small church in Marion, Indiana. After the wedding, Julia flew to Washington, D.C., to finish production on her comeback film, *The Pelican Brief.*

Over the next year and a half, Julia and Lyle went on with their careers. Unfortunately, those careers often kept them apart. They rarely spent more than a week at a time together. They also kept separate homes. Julia lived in New York City. Lyle lived in a small town in Texas. "We are pretending to be a normal couple," Julia told a reporter from *The New York Times.* Lyle added later, "We're just so happy to be together when we can be."

*Julia Roberts and Lyle Lovett.*

*The Pelican Brief* opened in late 1993. In it, Julia played a law student who comes up with a theory to explain the killing of two Supreme Court judges. The film was successful, and Julia was officially back in business. She made four more movies over the next year and a half. They were *I Love Trouble, Ready to Wear, Mary Reilly,* and *Game of Love.* Meanwhile, her husband spent most of his time on the road giving concerts.

The long separations created rumors in the tabloids about their relationship. Early on, the tabloids speculated that the marriage was in trouble. Julia and Lyle had been virtual strangers when they married. They had not spent enough time together since the marriage to stop being strangers. Those stories mixed with a report of Julia dancing closely with actor Ethan Hawke. Another story said Lyle had given Julia a private concert in Aspen, Colorado. Still another said the two had strolled hand-in-hand down the streets of Paris, France, during the *Ready to Wear* shoot.

*Julia Roberts at a news
conference talking about*
The Pelican Brief.

As her 30th birthday approached, Julia was on the verge of a new phase in her career.

The strain of the many separations finally took its toll. In March 1995, the couple announced they were separating. Julia was in London, England, filming *Mary Reilly*. The drama features Julia as the housekeeper for Dr. Jekyll and his dark side, Mr. Hyde. In the statement, the two said "We remain close and in great support of each other."

In a mirror of her personal life, Julia's career also floundered. *I Love Trouble, Game of Love, Mary Reilly,* and *Ready to Wear* all did poorly at the box office. In between, Julia enjoyed some success with *Something to Talk About* in 1995. The movie was about a woman who discovers her husband is having an affair. She also took time to travel to Haiti on behalf of the United Nations Children's Fund (UNICEF).

In 1996, critics applauded her performance in 1996's *Everyone Says I Love You*. She co-starred with Woody Allen in that movie. Yet as her 30th birthday approached, Julia was on the verge of a new phase in her career. It would be the best yet.

# BETTER
## THAN
# EVER

WITH HER DIVORCE BEHIND HER, A MORE
mature Julia was ready to get back to work. She
re-entered the spotlight with a splash in the 1997
hit *My Best Friend's Wedding*. In the film, Julia
plays a young woman whose longtime friend
announces he's getting married. Julia realizes she
loves him and doesn't want him to marry someone
else. She sets about seeing that the wedding never
happens. Julia's mother, Betty, appeared in the
movie as an extra.

*My Best Friend's Wedding* opened to the
highest-ever single weekend ticket sales for a
romantic comedy. It won Julia a Golden Globe
nomination for Best Performance by an Actress in
a Comedy/Musical. It also won her a People's
Choice Award for Favorite Motion Picture
Actress.

*Julia Roberts in a scene from* My Best Friend's Wedding.

Julia quickly followed that by starring opposite Mel Gibson in *Conspiracy Theory*. On the set, she displayed her usual fun-loving nature. Gibson sent her a freeze-dried rat on the first day of filming. She got revenge by putting clear plastic wrap over the seat of the toilet in his trailer.

*Conspiracy Theory* also did well in theaters. It and *Wedding* helped Julia win Harvard University's Hasty Pudding Woman of the Year Award in 1997.

In 1998, Julia took on several new challenges. In *Stepmom*, she played opposite Susan Sarandon and Ed Harris. She also was co-executive producer of the film along with Sarandon.

*Julia Roberts and Mel Gibson on the set of* Conspiracy Theory.

# Notting Hill

Also that year, she traveled to Africa to film a Public Broadcasting System documentary. It was called *In the Wild*. The following year, she teamed up with Hugh Grant to star as actress Anna Scott in *Notting Hill*. The part mirrored Julia's own life in that the media also hounded Anna. The film had Julia's character falling in love and settling down with ordinary guy Grant. Julia received another Golden Globe nomination for that role.

Julia quickly followed that success with *Runaway Bride*. *Bride* reunited her with her *Pretty Woman* co-star Richard Gere. It was about a woman who always leaves her fiancé at the altar.

# Runaway Bride

*Julia Roberts jams on a guitar at Harvard University's Hasty Pudding Theatre in Cambridge, Massachusetts. Julia was awarded the 1997 Hasty Pudding Woman of the Year.*

**Julia won a Primetime Emmy Award for her performance on *Law & Order*.**

In May 1999, Julia took on a guest role on the television series *Law & Order*. The show starred a promising young actor named Benjamin Bratt. Julia had met Benjamin several years before in Manhattan. Her performance on *Law & Order* earned her a Primetime Emmy Award. More importantly, it gave her more time with a man who was to be the next star in her personal life.

*Julia Roberts with Benjamin Bratt.*

# WILD **ABOUT**

# ERIN

AT AGE 32, JULIA ALREADY HAD ENJOYED more success than some actresses enjoy in an entire career. *Notting Hill* and *Runaway Bride* each had grossed more than $100 million in the United States alone. In fact, *Bride* was the sixth Julia Roberts film to top that earnings mark. Julia also had become the highest-paid actress in Hollywood. She was earning $17 million a film.

She shattered that record with her next project, *Erin Brockovich*. *Erin Brockovich* was based on the true story of a legal clerk who stops a utility company from polluting the water in her small California town. Julia earned a record $20 million to star in the movie. It was a long way from the $50,000 she earned as Daisy in *Mystic Pizza*. It also helped bring wages for female actresses closer to those typically enjoyed by male actors.

*Julia Roberts poses with the Golden Globe award she won for Best Actress for her role in Erin Brockovich.*

Julia Roberts is Erin Brockovich

Many critics said *Erin* was Julia's best work ever. She won another Golden Globe award for best actress, as well as an Oscar for her heroic, against-the-system performance. The real Erin Brockovich was known for her brashness, swearing, and short skirts. Julia brought all of that to life in a very believable way.

"She's the nicest movie mom I've ever met," said actor Scotty Leavenworth, who played Julia's son. "She very, extremely nice." Julia was known for telling jokes and goofing around with the crew on set. She especially enjoyed joking around with the younger actors.

"She came into the kids' trailers and let them go into hers," said Scotty's mother, Brenda. "At one point she told them, 'Oh, so you just come in and trash my trailer and then leave.' And they said, 'Yup.'" When not acting on-camera or clowning around off-camera, she was calling Bratt on his movie set in Los Angeles.

At the end of the year, Julia shifted gears and traveled to Mongolia. There she did another documentary for public broadcasting. This one was on wild horses. "She went for a week with no bath or shower, no proper toilet," said her director. "Yet she never complained."

Julia brought *Erin Brockovich* to life. She received her first-ever Oscar for her outstanding performance.

# OLDER

## AND WISER

JULIA RECENTLY GAVE AN INTERVIEW for *Good Housekeeping* magazine. Julia was asked what the biggest difference in her life was in her 30s versus 10 years before. "I weigh 20 pounds less and know 50 things more," she replied. She also talked about how she's learned to handle her celebrity status. "What's changed is my ability to express myself," she said. "I have more confidence now to speak up and say, 'You are crossing a line. …' " She certainly needs that confidence. The press has reported on virtually everything about her, including her weight to whether or not she shaves her underarms.

Now the media is seeking to learn more about her relationship with Bratt. The two spend much of their time together. Both enjoy sports such as jogging, inline skating, and bicycling. Between work, they alternate time between Julia's home in Manhattan and his home in San Francisco. (Julia also owns a 51-acre retreat near Taos, New Mexico.) Rumors of a marriage in the future abound, but as of yet, they are unconfirmed.

Julia maintains her girl-next-door lifestyle by jogging through the streets of New York and even taking the public bus. Her agent, Elaine Goldsmith-Thomas, told *PEOPLE Magazine* that Julia is always encouraging her to do it as well. "She always says to me, 'Just hop a bus.' She does it, and she's flabbergasted that I don't."

She remains close to her mother and sister as well. A dispute with her older brother, Eric, has strained relations between the two of them. However, Julia still spends time with Eric's daughter, her eight-year-old niece Emma.

In her spare time, Julia enjoys cooking and knitting. "I learned (knitting) from a lovely guy who was the standby painter on *The Pelican Brief*," she said. "As a result, every movie I go on, I sit knitting, and people come up and say, 'Oh, I want to know how to knit.' By the end of the movie, there's always a knitting circle that has grown."

*Julia Roberts at the 2001 awards dinner of the Los Angeles Film Critics Association. Julia was voted Best Actress by the association for her role in* Erin Brokovich.

Meanwhile, she now has her own film production company in New York. It's called Shoelace Productions. "I have a great appreciation for movies across the board," she says. "Even if they stink, I can sit there and say, ' I see a good effort there. I can see the try, I can see the attempt even though it fell a little short of the mark.' Because it's just not easy to make a movie."

When not making movies, she's often seen racing between her Manhattan apartment and the Shoelace office. Usually, she's wearing sweats and no make-up.

"There are people who see me at the grocery store and think that I should be wearing Chanel or something," Julia says. "They can't respond to the fact that I'm in cut-offs and a T-shirt. As if it's part of my job to always look impeccable. Which isn't ever gonna happen."

*Julia Roberts accepts her award for Favorite Motion Picture Actress during the People's Choice Awards January 7, 2001, in Pasadena, California.*

# FLASH
## THAT
# SMILE

PEOPLE SEEM DRAWN TO JULIA ON AND
off the set. Steven Soderbergh, who directed her in
*Erin*, puts it this way. "Julia is touched by
something, a zest and life force you just want to be
around. She became a huge star early, which a lot
of people don't survive. She's managed to get
through it with her soul intact."

Off the set, fans often approach Julia. "This
happens rather frequently," she says. "Someone
comes up and asks, 'Are you Julia Roberts?' and I
say yes and they say, 'No you're not,' and I say
yes and they say no. After that I just kind of let
it go."

Movie offers continue to role in for Hollywood's hottest leading lady. She's been approached about starring in a remake of the Alfred Hitchcock classic *To Catch A Thief.* Her director in *Erin Brockovich* has pegged Julia for the all-star remake of *Ocean's 11.* She also has been mentioned for another remake, this one with Meg Ryan. It's called *The Women.* In summer 2000, she was in Mexico filming *The Mexican* with Brad Pitt. *The Mexican* hit theaters in March of 2001. The movie was another big hit for Julia.

Even Julia's old school, Campbell High, has honored her. The school now has a full theater curriculum. Each year, there's a prize for the most promising student in that curriculum. The prize is the Julia Roberts Award.

When it comes to the future, Julia is not one to spend much time plotting what the years ahead will bring. "If you're so busy thinking about 10 years from now, suddenly you'll be there and you won't remember anything you did for the last 10 years to get there," she says.

Whatever her next moves are, it's likely that Julia's fans will be treated to more of her dazzling smile and big laugh. "I love what I do," she says. "I'd do it for free."

*Julia Roberts backstage showing off her 26th Annual People's Choice Award for Favorite Motion Picture Actress.*

# WHERE ON THE WEB?

You can find out more about Julia Roberts by visiting the following web sites.

**America's Sweetheart: Julia Roberts**
http//www2.netdoor.com/~cplowe/julia.htm

**Starring Julia Roberts**
http://starringjuliaroberts.cjb.net/

**Information on Julia Roberts**
http://www.geocities.com/Paris/4097/julia.html

**JuliaRobertsOnline.com (official site)**
http://www.juliarobertsonline.com/

Fans also can write to Julia at:
Ms. Julia Roberts
C/O International Creative Management
8942 Wilshire Boulevard
Beverly Hills, California 90211

# GLOSSARY

**Producer:** the person on a movie crew who handles the details of getting the movie funded, filmed, and completed.

**Tabloids:** newspapers that print stories on gossip and rumors.

**United Nations Children's Fund:** an international not-for-profit group that seeks to help children around the world.

# INDEX

**A**
Africa  42
Allen, Woody  37
Aspen, Colorado  34

**B**
*Baja Oklahoma*  14
Barstow, California
    4
*Blood Red*  12, 14
Bratt, Benjamin  44

**C**
Calcutta, India  29
Campbell High
    School  12, 58
Click modeling
    agency  12
*Conspiracy Theory*
    40
*Crime Story*  14

**D**
Dame, Gerry  4
Day-Lewis, Daniel
    29
*Dying Young*  24

**E**
*Everyone Says I Love
    You*  37
*Erin Brockovich*  4,
    46, 48, 56, 58

**F**
Fitzhugh Lee
    Elementary
    School  11
*Flatliners*  20, 23

**G**
*Game of Love*  34, 37
Gibson, Mel  40
Golden Globe
    Awards  16, 19,
    38, 42, 48
Goldsmith-Thomas,
    Elaine  52
*Good Housekeeping*
    50
Grant, Hugh  42

**H**
Haiti  37
Harling, Robert  16
Harris, Ed  40
Harvard University
    40
Hawke, Ethan  34
HBO  14
Hitchcock, Alfred
    58
*Hook*  24

**I**
*I Love Trouble*  34,
    37
*In the Wild*  42

**J**
Julia Roberts Award
    58

**L**
*Law & Order*  44
Leavenworth, Brenda
    48
Leavenworth, Scotty
    48
Lenwood Elementary
    School  4
London, England  37
Los Angeles,
    California  48
Lovett, Lyle  32, 34

**M**
Manhattan, New
    York  44, 50, 54
Marion, Indiana  32
Marshall, Gary  16
*Mary Reilly*  34, 37
McDermott, Dylan
    23
Mongolia  48
Mother Teresa  29
*My Best Friend's
    Wedding*  38
*Mystic Pizza*  14, 46

**N**
NBC-TV  14
Neeson, Liam  14, 23

New York City  12,
    32, 52, 54
*Notting Hill*  42, 46

**O**
*Ocean's 11*  58
Oscar  12, 16, 19, 48

**P**
Paris, France  34
Patric, Jason  23, 24,
    29
Penn, Sean  29
*PEOPLE Magazine*
    6, 52
People's Choice
    Award  38
Pitt, Brad  58
*Pretty Woman*  19,
    20, 42
Primetime Emmy
    Award  44
Public Broadcasting
    System  42, 48

**R**
*Ready to Wear*  34,
    37
Roberts, Betty  8, 11
Roberts, Emma  52
Roberts, Eric  8, 12,
    52
Roberts, Lisa  8, 12
Roberts, Walter  8,
    11
*Runaway Bride*  42,
    46
*Runaway Train*  12
Ryan, Meg  58

**S**
San Francisco,
    California  50
Sarandon, Susan  40
*Satisfaction*  14, 23
Schumacher, Joel  20
*Shakespeare in Love*
    29
Shoelace Produc-
    tions  54

*Sleeping With the
    Enemy*  20
Smyrna, Georgia  8
Soderbergh, Steven
    56
*Something to Talk
    About*  37
Spielberg, Steven  24
*Steel Magnolias*  14,
    16, 19, 23
*Stepmom*  40
Sutherland, Donald
    20
Sutherland, Kiefer
    20, 23, 24

**T**
Taos, New Mexico
    50
Texas  32
*The Mexican*  58
*The New York Times*
    32
*The Pelican Brief*
    32, 34, 52
*The Player*  29
*The Women*  58
*To Catch A Thief*  58

**U**
UNICEF  37

**W**
Walt Disney
    Company  16
Washington, D.C.  32